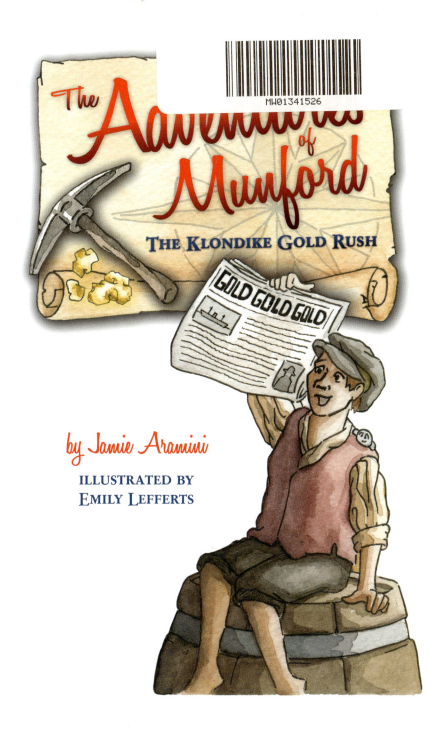

The Adventures of Munford
THE KLONDIKE GOLD RUSH

Written by Jamie Aramini
Illustrated by Emily Lefferts
Munford character and concepts created by George Wiggers

© 2010 Jamie Aramini and George Wiggers. All Rights Reserved. No part of this publication may be copied or reproduced in any form or by any means without permission in writing from the publisher.

First Edition

Library of Congress Control Number: 2010925576
ISBN: 987-1-931397-66-7
Published in the U.S.A. by Geography Matters, Inc.®
800-426-4650
www.geomatters.com

Printed in the United States of America

Dedication

For Joey and James

Acknowledgements

Thanks to Josh and Cindy Wiggers for trusting me with your dream of Munford. I am honored to have the privilege to write this book.

Table of Contents

Chapter One:	SEATTLE	7
Chapter Two:	GETTING READY	19
Chapter Three:	ALL ABOARD	27
Chapter Four:	SKAGWAY	37
Chapter Five:	DYEA	49
Chapter Six:	ALEX MCDONALD	59
Chapter Seven:	THE GOLDEN STAIRCASE	69
Chapter Eight:	LAKE BENNETT	79
Chapter Nine:	THE WHITEHORSE RAPIDS	89
Chapter Ten:	DAWSON CITY	99
Chapter Eleven:	GOLD DUST	109
Chapter Twelve:	PANNING FOR GOLD	119
Chapter Thirteen:	NUGGETS OF GOLD	127

Epilogue:	A NOTE FROM GRANDPA GILBERT	135
The Klondike Gold Rush:	FASCINATING FACTS	139
Author's Note:	SHARING THE VISION OF MUNFORD	140

Chapter One
SEATTLE

"Extra! Extra! Read all about it!" A newspaper boy shouted from the street corner. I worked my way closer to him.

"Gold! Gold! Gold! Gold!" the headline read. "The steamship *Portland* arrives today with nearly a ton of gold," I read from the smaller print below the headline.

Gold. I think I heard that word a hundred times today. It is the talk of the town. It doesn't matter where I am. The store clerk, the bank teller, the stable boy—everybody has got gold on the brain.

I wanted to know more, so I floated over to the seaport. When the *Portland* docked, I would have more answers.

Have you ever been to a seaport? It is a busy place. There are lots of boats and people. Things are being unloaded from some boats, while other boats are just getting packed to head out to sea.

You have to squeeze your way through all the people. Many of them are there to say goodbye to someone who is setting sail. Some are there trying to barter for a ticket so they can set out on an adventure of their own.

There are animals everywhere: dogs, cats, chickens in cages getting loaded onto boats—and the fish! The whole place stinks of fish. Some of the boats sell the day's catch right there on the dock.

As you can tell, a seaport is usually a busy place. Today, this one was even busier. It looked like everyone in town had come to watch for the *Portland's* arrival. Everyone wanted to see it for themselves.

Not in a long time had anything this exciting happened in Seattle. Did I tell you that I'm describing Seattle, Washington? Do you know where that is? The first time I heard of it, I thought it was part of Washington, D.C. Turns out I was wrong about that.

Seattle

Washington is a state on the other side of the country from Washington D.C. Seattle is a city inside of Washington state. All of those Washingtons can really be confusing. Just look on a map and it should clear things up.

Let's get back to the subject at hand. The Seattle seaport was hopping with people. It was July 1897, but no one seemed to mind the warm summer weather. Times were tough in this small town. Washington had only been a state for a few years, so the economy was still getting established. A good job and a steady income were hard to get. Most people were just barely getting by. Now you understand why gold had caused such a frenzy!

The *Portland*, fresh from the Alaskan coast, would dock soon. "A million dollars worth of gold," I overheard someone say. I had never heard of so much gold, and I guess I wasn't the only one. Thousands of people pushed their way down to the docks to see it for themselves. There was a feeling of hope in the air. Everyone wondered if heading north and looking for gold might be the answer to their problems.

As the *Portland* docked, the crowd pushed closer for a better look. Huge wooden crates were stacked on the ship. Armed guards stood by as the passengers disembarked. "Disembark" is just a fancy word that means they were getting off of the ship.

"Is it true?" someone from the crowd shouted. "Is there really a ton of gold on that ship?"

"I'm afraid you've been misinformed," said one of the passengers with a raised voice. The crowd went silent. "I'd say there's probably closer to two tons." With that, he let out a cheer. The rest of the passengers cheered along with him. Soon the crowd joined in.

Two tons of gold! I slipped away from the crowd. An idea was starting to form in my mind, and I knew just whom I needed to talk to about it— my Grandpa Gilbert. He would be able to tell me everything I needed to know about gold and what I could do to get some of my own.

You might remember Grandpa from one of my other adventures. He is someone I can always count on to give me advice. Of course, he isn't really my grandfather. I am a water molecule, after all. All of us water molecules are the same age. We just get recycled through the water cycle again and again. We don't have family like you do, either. I just call Gilbert "Grandpa" because he is a wise explorer, famous for his travels in the world of water molecules.

Lucky for me, Grandpa was in Seattle. He had blown in with a thunderstorm just last week. Now he was hanging out in a watering trough over in the center of town. I hitched a ride on a nearby horse, hoping it would stop for a drink so I could talk to Grandpa.

When we arrived at the trough, I slipped down into the water with a drip of the horse's sweat. (Kind of gross, I know.) As soon as I spotted Grandpa, I told him everything I knew. I was so excited that it came out in a bit of a jumble, "Gold…Klondike…*Portland*… Two tons!"

"Whoa there! Slow down," Grandpa said. "You're talking too fast."

I repeated my story, slowly this time. When I got to the part about the two tons, Grandpa interrupted me. "So it is true then? Two tons of gold. That sure will change things around here."

I had a silly question. I really hated to ask it, but I needed to know. "What exactly is gold, Grandpa?"

"Gold is just a metal," he answered.

"Why all the fuss, then?"

"Because it is a valuable metal. It is pretty hard to come by, which makes it worth a lot. It is used as money."

I had more questions about this metal. "Where does it come from?" I asked.

Grandpa was quick to answer, "The ground. There are tiny little bits of it in most soil."

What? You could find gold in most soil? "I better start digging!"

Grandpa laughed. "Hang on there. I said there are tiny bits of gold. What you are looking for is a gold deposit—a place where there is a lot of gold."

I was starting to get impatient. "Where would that be?"

"Well, there are gold deposits all over the world—South Africa, New Zealand, Australia, California. Most of them, though, have already been mined. The trick is to find a place that hasn't yet been mined. The gold that was on the *Portland* came from Canada, from a region called the Klondike. There are already a few mines set up there, but there could still be some gold left to discover."

This was just what I needed to hear. "Grandpa! Come on! We need to get to the Klondike and fast!"

He laughed a big laugh. "And that's why it's called a gold rush."

"A gold rush?" I thought I had heard the term before, but I couldn't remember.

"This is when big groups of people hurry to look for gold. It's a rush of people in a rush to find gold," Grandpa smiled.

I definitely wanted to be a part of the rush. I had gold fever! "What do you say, Gramps? Will you come to the Klondike with me and join the gold rush?"

"I'm afraid you'll have to go this one alone, Munford. I've been part of a gold rush before. It isn't as much fun as it sounds, you know."

I sensed a story coming on. Grandpa Gilbert had a good story for every occasion. "Another gold rush? Where? When?"

Grandpa leaned back in the rocking chair and took a deep breath. He closed his eyes. I could tell he was remembering. "It was 1849. The first bits of gold dust were found in southern California. Pretty soon someone had found whole nuggets. It wasn't long before folks from all over—including me—were headed to California to find a piece of their own. Of course, there isn't much a water molecule like me or you can do with gold. Even so, it sure is easy to get swept up in the adventure of it all." Grandpa sighed.

"Forty-niners, we were called. There were so many of us! Everyone needed supplies and food and a place to sleep. It was a mess. You could hardly afford to buy a donkey out there. By the time I arrived, most of the good spots had already been taken. People were killing each other over 'em, too. What a mess."

"A mess. Yes. I think you already said that. What about the gold?" Sometimes you had to steer Grandpa in the right direction to get the answer you wanted.

"Oh, right. The gold. I found a few small bits. Not even enough to cover the cost of my supplies. I did meet some nice people, though, a lot of scoundrels, too. If they couldn't find any gold of their own, some seemed content to steal whatever they could to make up for it!"

So Grandpa hadn't found gold after all. It would be different for me. It wasn't 1849 anymore. Not to mention I would be in Canada, not California. Surely I would find something.

Grandpa left me with a few parting words. "It will be quite an adventure, Munford. Be careful whom you trust. Sometimes people get all wrapped up in gold fever and forget their manners. You better get moving, though! Every moment wasted is a gold claim lost."

He didn't have to tell me twice. I was ready to go, but how would I get out of the trough? Soon enough, the horse took another big drink of the water, lapping me up with it. I held on to his lips with all my might. I didn't want to get stuck in his stomach, that's for sure! I kept holding on to his lips as the horse and his owner trotted down the street, taking me with them.

Chapter Two
GETTING READY

As I looked around the streets of Seattle, I noticed that things were a little busy. There were more people out and about than usual. I dropped off the horse when I spotted the general store. A huge advertisement read, "Get Your Gold Supplies Here! Best Selection in Town!"

Once inside, I was glad to be a water molecule. The entire town of Seattle, it seemed, was shopping today. There was hardly room for the humans to squeeze through the aisles. Were all of these people headed to the Klondike? Were all of these people searching for gold? It was still early in the day and many of the shelves were already empty.

"Do you have any wool socks?" a man asked the clerk.

"I'm afraid not. We just sold out an hour ago. I do have these nice, new light-weight socks." He held up a pair of socks so thin, you could almost see through them. "They keep the air circulating around your feet."

The man frowned. "No, those won't do. I need heavy wool socks, not lightweight. My feet will freeze off in the Klondike!"

A young woman overheard the conversation and stepped up to the counter. "I'll take all the socks you've got left. Light-weight or not."

The clerk was very happy about this, but the man grew agitated. "Now just wait a minute. I didn't say I wasn't going to buy them. I guess I could layer the socks if I had to. I'll take them."

The clerk, bagging up the socks, was confused now. "But, sir, the lady has already agreed to purchase the socks. I have to sell them to her. I do have some wool yarn. Perhaps you could knit your own socks." Some of the customers snickered at this.

The man, unwilling to accept defeat, turned to the woman. "I'll buy your socks. Twice the price you paid for them."

GETTING READY

She took her bag of socks from the clerk and turned to the exit. "I'm sorry. I must have these socks. My husband and I leave for the Klondike in the morning. We mustn't get frostbite." With that, she walked out, her bag clutched tightly under her arm.

The clerk apologized to the male customer. "Perhaps you might check with the other stores."

"I've been to all the stores. All the supplies are selling out quickly. I just need some extra socks. I don't have enough to make the trip."

A little old lady stepped up to the counter, putting down some fabric to purchase. As the clerk added up her bill, she turned to the sock man. "I'll sell you my husband's socks."

"Really?" he asked.

"Yes. Three times the cost of a new pair."

"Three times! That's robbery! I'll lose my toes before I pay that."

The woman gathered up her purchases. "Fine then. My husband will be glad to keep his socks." She turned to the door.

"Twice the cost of a new pair," the man called out to her.

She turned back. "Throw in a spool of yarn and it's a deal."

"Done." The man was pleased to finally purchase some socks. The little old lady was happy to make some money. I'm glad I wasn't around to hear her husband when he found out that she had sold his socks!

The store clerk posted a list of supplies needed for a trip to the Klondike. It has been published in the paper that morning. It was quite long, and included the following items, among other things: medical supplies, several sets of very warm clothes,

GETTING READY

extra socks, 150 pounds bacon, 400 pounds flour, 20 pounds coffee, and 20 pounds salt. I don't know about you, but that sounds like a lot of work, hauling around all that food.

The clerk told us that getting to the gold required a five hundred mile trip down a river. "Are you saying we need to buy a boat?" a customer asked, clearly concerned.

The clerk laughed. He must have thought that we were all crazy, buying up socks and wanting to find gold. "You can't buy a boat. You'll never get it up and over the Coast Mountains into Canada. It will be hard enough to get all of the supplies you need without adding all the extra weight."

"What will we do then?"

"The people from the *Portland* said that they built their own boats once they got to the headwaters of the river. You'll have to do the same. I have a fine selection of tools to aid you in building a boat. You need a saw and ax to bring down a tree…" He continued to list all the tools needed as the customers grabbed them off the shelves in a hurry. Before long, there wasn't a hammer or nail left!

"Is there anything else we'll need?" someone shouted over the noisy crowd.

The clerk looked around. His shelves were mostly empty now. The remaining goods looked like they had just been thrown down by the shoppers. The whole store was in a mess. He turned to a glass case along the wall and pointed. "You're going to need a gun."

"A gun? What on earth for?" asked a woman.

"Maybe he thinks we'll need to shoot the gold!" said someone else.

Everyone got a good laugh out of that. The clerk didn't think it was too funny. "Don't be foolish. You are going to need a gun. For one thing, you'll need it for hunting. You might be able to catch yourself some wild game. Give you something to eat when all that bacon runs out. And then there's the other thing…" No one was talking now. What other thing could he be talking about?

"Greed. Let's say you find a big gold nugget. You go to file your claim, but before you even make it there, your next-door neighbor shoots you dead and takes your gold. It happens all the time out there in the wild. With a gun, you'll be able to protect yourself and protect your claim."

He was a convincing salesman. "How much?"

"Double the price on the tags," the clerk replied. I guess he figured if it could work for socks, it could work for guns, too. I turned to leave. I wasn't going to be a part of this price gouging. I didn't need a gun anyway. No one is going to shoot a water molecule.

I'm sorry, what was that? Oh, you didn't? It must have slipped my mind. Sometimes I completely forget to mention that I'm a water molecule. I am made of two parts hydrogen and one part oxygen. I come in many different forms—rain, snow, fog, sleet, ice, steam, cloud, river, and ocean. You get the idea.

Did I even tell you my name? I am Munford. I am an adventurer and an explorer. I always like to be where the action is. Maybe you have been on one of my adventures before. I am glad you have decided to come along with me this time. The more people that come along, the more fun it will be! I can't wait for us to explore the Klondike together.

Let's get out of this store and head down to the docks. I won't be buying many supplies at these prices anyway! It shouldn't take long to find a ship to take me to Alaska.

Chapter Three
All Aboard!

The streets of Seattle weren't the only the places full of action today. The seaport was just as busy. The docks were covered up with people. Finding a ship to take me to the Klondike was easier said than done. Everyone was looking to book passage to Alaska. From there, they would make the long trek to the Klondike where their gold awaited. How would I ever find a ship to board amidst all these people?

People weren't the only thing cluttering up the docks. There was a lot of cargo as well—trunks, crates, bags. Everywhere you turned there were stacks and stacks of supplies waiting to be loaded onto the ships. No wonder all of the stores were empty.

Not everyone, though, had purchased all of the necessary supplies for the trip. Some of them simply couldn't find what they needed since most of the stores had sold out of everything. Others couldn't afford to buy supplies and buy their ticket, so they just bought the ticket and made do with what they had. Some of them boarded the boats with nothing but the clothes on their back!

I remembered Grandpa Gilbert's warnings about high prices during the '49 Gold Rush. I imagined that things would only be worse in the isolated Klondike. Not to mention that things would be colder, a lot colder. No one was thinking about that, though. They only had one thing on their minds, and that was gold. The weather wasn't important to them just yet. It wouldn't be long, though, before they felt how foolish they had been. I saw a few people that I recognized, which wasn't surprising. Most of Seattle was there. The barber, a local farmer, even the librarian—no one was immune from gold fever.

"Mayor Wood put in his resignation," I overheard someone say.

"The mayor? Of Seattle? Whatever for?" replied another.

"Gold. I guess he thinks he can make more in the mines than he can running the city. Seems a bit foolish if you ask me." I thought it odd that someone would call the mayor a fool when they themselves had left their jobs to head to the Klondike.

Most of the people at the docks were men, but there were quite a few women as well. I hopped onto the dress sleeve of one such woman. I was interested to know why she was heading to the Klondike.

She must have already bought her ticket. She wasted no time bartering with the captains like many did. Instead, she walked straight toward one of the ships. A sign outside the ship read, "Head for Alaska and Join the Klondike Gold Rush! Set Sail Today!"

Now was my chance! I held onto to the woman's sleeve as she walked up the wooden planks and onto the boat. I was excited to finally be headed to the Klondike.

The woman seemed excited as well. "My name is Belinda Mulroney," she announced to the men on deck. Most of the men paid no attention to her, although a few gave their names as well.

"My name is Charles," replied one of the gentlemen.

"Where are you from?" asked Belinda politely.

"Seattle." Charles, a skinny man with round glasses, seemed nervous. He was dressed in shabby clothes that were so thin, you might have seen through them if the light was right. I wondered to myself if he would ever make it in the freezing temperatures we would soon be facing. "I'm from

Scranton, Pennsylvania," she said. "But I've traveled all over. What brings you to Alaska?"

Charles smiled. "The gold rush, of course. I've sold my farm, used the cash to buy supplies, and now I hope to strike gold and make it rich."

"I hope to 'make it rich' as well," said Belinda.

Charles scoffed. "Make it rich? A woman? Ha. Do you have no man traveling with you?"

Belinda frowned, "Well, no, actually, I—"

"No man! You'll never make it the Klondike. Maybe if you ask one of the captains, they will have the decency to refund you your money. You had best get off the ship and stay in Seattle."

She was upset now. "I'll do no such thing! Why, I have just as much right to make money as you or any man!"

"Rights have nothing to do with it. A woman can't mine for gold. It is hard labor. Nothing fit for a lady like yourself."

Belinda put her hands on her hips. "I have no intention on mining for gold. Only a foolish man—like you—would waste time on that. It's a silly fantasy and no reason to sell your farm! I intend on making it rich by selling supplies to the miners."

Charles had a good laugh at that. "Oh, a little business woman! What a joke. Now, if you'll excuse me, I need to check and make sure my luggage has been safely stowed on board." With that, he walked away, leaving a very angry Belinda behind.

I didn't understand why Charles had been so rude. Belinda's plan sounded like a good one to me. In fact, Belinda was one of the very few people on the boat who had a plan at all. Some hoped to get jobs at an already existing mine until they could

find gold on their own. A few men had pooled their money to purchas mining equipment. They planned to use it or sell it when they arrive. Most, however, were just feeling lucky. They had seen the *Portland* and its passengers; laden with gold, and hoped that good fortune would smile on them as well. I thought a plan like Belinda's would be much better than no plan at all.

There were so many people on the ship that it started to get very warm. So warm, in fact, that I evaporated. Pretty soon I was just a vapor in the air. I left Belinda to have a look around. The ship was truly buzzing with excitement. I overheard conversation after conversation about gold. Where were the best places to look? How did one file a gold claim? How would you spend all the money? These were just some of the things being discussed.

I sat at one round table with a group of men, each telling what they were going to do with their gold fortune. "I'll finally marry my sweetheart," said one young man. "Her father thinks I'm a poor, lazy good-for-nothing. When I come home with my pockets full of gold, why, he'll think different!"

One older gentleman let out a chuckle. "Don't waste ye money on women, lad! You'll soon be broke again." He pulled at his white beard with his hand. "Me, I'm going to travel the world before I die. See all the exotic places."

"Well, you better hurry up old man!" Everyone laughed.

Another man spoke up. "I don't need much gold, just enough to buy a little farm and some livestock. I'll just give the rest away."

"You can give it to me, then!" Someone said, followed by a round of "Yes!" from the others.

Everyone was in high spirits. It must have been the thought of all that gold just waiting to be found. I overheard some people striking up business deals and partnerships. All around the ship, kindness in action could be seen. Everyone wanted to help everyone else.

"If I make it rich, I'll help all of you find gold of your own," someone said.

"I have some extra socks that I can give you," said another.

"I'm a doctor," said one very tall man. "If anyone needs medical care, I'll be more than happy to provide it."

"I'm a lawyer," said the man next to him. "I can help everyone file their gold claims."

"There will be plenty of gold to go around! I hear the streets are paved with it!" said one of the deck hands.

"Please have my seat, ma'am," a gentleman said to a now calm Belinda Mulroney.

With this great group of people, my trip to the Klondike was going to be a lot of fun. Grandpa Gilbert had told me about all the scoundrels during the 1849 Gold Rush. It looked like that wouldn't be a problem this time around, no, sir. Everyone was as nice as could be.

We had a quick stop to make before we reached our final stop of Dyea, Alaska. We had to drop off a few of the passengers in Skagway, another Alaskan town. Of course, Alaska was still not a state. The United States had purchased the land only thirty years before. I was anxious to see what the area was like.

Chapter Four
SKAGWAY

It took a little longer to get to Skagway than I had expected. The ship's captain and crew had never been there before. To make matters worse, they couldn't even find it on their maps. They were traveling solely using directions from someone in Seattle. I found out later that we were one of the lucky ships. We did end up making it there. Some ships with passengers bound for the Klondike went around for weeks in search of Skagway before finally giving up and going back home.

Everyone rushed to the ship's deck when the crew announced that we had arrived in Skagway. I looked over the edge of the ship, surprised at what I saw. There was no dock in sight, only beach.

"Where is the dock?" asked one of the passengers.

"Well…there isn't one, I'm afraid," replied a crewmember.

"No dock? How will we unload our things?"

The crewmember shuffled his feet. "I'm sorry, but your luggage will be unloaded directly onto the beach." He held up his hand to stop the murmuring that rose up from the crowd. "Skagway is a new town. No ship has ever needed to dock here until recently, when the gold was found in the Klondike. They just haven't built a dock yet."

There was a lot of whining amongst the passengers. No one wanted to unload on the beach, but they ended up doing just that. They weren't giving up that easily on the gold.

It was a nice change of pace to be back on land. I was still a vapor, which made it easy for me to float into town on the ocean breeze.

On the surface, Skagway seemed like a nice town. It was at the base of a trail into the Klondike called White Pass. The town was overflowing with people preparing to head out in search of gold.

The first building I saw was the telegraph office. A sign out front read, "Send news to loved ones back home! Telegraphs, only $5.00. Soapy Smith, Proprietor."

A line of people twisted out onto the street. Everyone wanted to tell their families back in Seattle that they had arrived safely. Now, five dollars seemed a little steep to me. I had to remind myself that a gold rush was going on. Of course prices would be a little high. The temperature was cooler now that I was off the over packed boat. I condensed on the side of a woman's bag as she waited in line.

I stayed with her as she waited and waited and waited. I passed the time by watching people. Just like the ship, Skagway had a wide variety of people. Some of the people were returning from the White Pass Trail. For the most part, they looked a little beat up and worn out. Only a very few appeared to have struck gold. You could tell because their arms were full of new packages and they held their heads up high.

We were moving further up the line, getting closer to the office entrance. We rested next to a tall telegraph pole. It was connected to another pole by telegraph wire. Poles and wires, connected just like these, stretched all the way back to Seattle. The messages would travel along those wires to the telegraph office in Seattle.

    As I stared at the poles, I noticed something peculiar. Only a few hundred feet from the telegraph office, the poles stopped. I squinted my eyes to be sure. Yep, it was true! This telegraph line didn't stretch to Seattle. It didn't even reach the end of the Skagway city limits. It was a scam. "Soapy Smith, Proprietor" was nothing more than a con artist.

    Everyone was so excited to get to send a telegram. They hadn't even noticed the shortage of poles. I needed to head to the sheriff's office. I had to alert them to this scam. But how would I get there?

    A fly landed beside me, and I knew just what to do. I jumped on to the fly and held on as it flew away. I looked up and down the street, but saw no sign of any law enforcement. The fly flew right through the front doors of the general store. It landed on the counter and I jumped off. Whew! What a ride.

    I hoped that I might find the sheriff in the store. This wasn't the case. It became obvious that I

had interrupted something. "I…I…I just don't have it this week," stammered the store manager. He was surrounded by a group of rough looking men.

"Soapy isn't going to be happy about this," said one of the men. "You know that you have to pay Soapy a part of your weekly profits."

The manager pulled out a ledger. "Look!" He pointed. "These records show what I've made. My shipments have been late. My bills are all past due. I haven't made any profit this month."

The men didn't even glance at the ledger. One of them grabbed the manager by the arm and gave it a good twist. "We'll be back, tomorrow. You better have the money or we will have to contact the sheriff. He'll be more than happy to arrest you if Soapy asks."

I gasped. Even the sheriff was corrupt in Skagway. It seemed that this fellow Soapy Smith was into everybody's business. Where would I find help to defeat the evil Soapy Smith?

When someone purchased a sack of flour, I held on as they walked out of the store.

"I'm looking for city hall," someone on the street asked.

"Three blocks to the east," came the reply. "Or go to Jeff Smith's Saloon. There's the real city hall."

City hall! That would be a good place to start my search for justice. I was confused about what the man had said. A saloon as city hall? I couldn't make sense of it, but I decided to check it out. I leaped onto the man's hat.

He found Jeff Smith's Saloon a few blocks over. We went into the place, which was dimly lit. A huge photograph of a creepy looking man hung on the wall. Below it was a small sign, "Jeff 'Soapy' Smith, Proprietor." Now I knew what the man on the street had meant. Soapy was the real boss of the town, and the saloon was his headquarters. This was where he managed all of his criminal activities.

This seemed like as good a place as any to get information. The man sat down at one of the tables. "Soapy Smith is a lying, cheating—" a man began.

"Shh!" said the man sitting next to him. "Don't let one of his men hear you! They'll get you for sure."

"Why bother?" he replied. "Soapy's already taken every-thing I own with his so-called 'taxes.' I've got nothing left."

"Tell me about it," whispered his friend. "I sold everything I owned to come to the Klondike and Soapy beat me out of it all the first night I was here. I thought I was just playing a friendly game of poker, but Soapy and his men tricked me into gambling away everything."

Things were out of control. Soapy Smith had overtaken the town of Skagway. This man was getting rich without having to mine for gold!

Suddenly, it occurred to me. I might be in danger. It was obvious that Soapy would do whatever it took to get what he wanted. I decided I wouldn't stick around to find out what that was. I needed to head back toward the ship, and fast.

I slid down the man's arm and onto the floor. I gripped onto the first boot that was going towards the exit. We headed down the street, squeezing through the people. We passed the general store with its slow business. We walked by the telegraph office with its long, twisting lines. Then, out of the corner of my eye, I saw him.

Soapy Smith! There he was, in person, just a few feet away from me. I shivered. He looked more evil in person than he did in his picture back in the saloon.

I looked around for a place to hide. There was nowhere to go! Where could I go? What could I do? He had already spotted me and was heading my way.

My best bet was just to blend in and hope he would lose sight of me. I slipped into a nearby mud puddle. He was getting closer now, scanning the

Skagway

streets for any sign of me. What would I do if he asked me for money? I didn't have any! I was a goner for sure.

He walked right up to the puddle with a grimace on his face. I stayed as quiet as I could. Would my muddy disguise work? He leaned down and looked right in the puddle. I closed my eyes in fright. I just knew this would be the end of Munford.

"Soapy! Come quick! There's a fight at the saloon!" One of Soapy's cronies shouted from across the street. He jumped up and walked away.

I let out a huge sigh of relief. I was going to make it out of Skagway, after all. As soon as Soapy was out of sight, I caught a ride back to the ship. Skagway certainly wasn't what I had expected. I wanted no part of the evil going on there. I hoped that Dyea would be better.

I worried about all the people headed for Skagway. They had no idea what awaited them. They wouldn't believe it if someone told them! An evil gangster named Soapy Smith? It just sounded too strange to be true, but I had seen it with my own eyes. Soapy Smith was real. I didn't rest until we were

safely on our way to our final stop, Dyea, Alaska—
far away from Soapy and his men. Let's hope things
would be better in this new city.

Chapter Five
DYEA

Dyea was only a few miles from Skagway, but there was a big difference between the two cities—there was no Soapy Smith in Dyea. Dyea was a smaller town, but it was overrun with people setting off in search for gold. I felt lost in the swirl of excitement.

"Get your pack horses here!" shouted a man on the street. "Get 'em before we run out! Two weeks before another load comes in!" Of course, I hadn't even thought about needing a packhorse. How else would people get their supplies up and over the mountains?

"Get out of my way, lady!" a man pushed a woman aside as he made his way to the line to buy a horse.

The woman lost her balance and fell to the ground. No one stopped to help her up. Everyone was too busy elbowing and pushing their way further up the horse line. "How much for the horse?"

The salesmen held a packhorse by the reigns. "For this fine specimen, five hundred dollars."

"Five hundred dollars! That's criminal! I could buy the animal for a quarter of the price back home."

"Take it or leave it, sir. If you don't buy it, someone else will." He bought it and led it away.

With a swirl of wind, I took one last glance back at the crowd, still pushing and shoving for a chance to buy a horse. It reminded me of something I had overheard one of the natives say. He wasn't very happy with all of these people taking over his town. It didn't help that everyone was so rude. He had called them "stampeders." After my experience with the horse crowd, I understood why he chose that term. These people were like an angry herd of cattle stampeding through Dyea, trying to get to the gold. I heard the term "stampeder" a few more times on my journey. It was a name that stuck for the people of the Klondike Gold Rush.

I needed to find a companion to travel with up the mountain. Luckily, I found myself at a local hotel. Folks would need a rest after the chaos at Skagway and the long boat ride.

A large sign that said "No Vacancies" hung from the front door. A handwritten note below it said, "ABSOLUTELY POSITIVELY NO VACANCIES." I wasn't really sure what the word "vacancies" meant, so I listened to the man at the desk.

"I'm sorry, sir. If you read the sign, you'll see that we have no vacancies." The clerk spoke in a soft, slow voice.

"Yes, I read the sign," said the man at the counter. "I read it, but I just wanted to check and be sure. Will you have any opening up soon?"

The clerk sighed. "Abbbsssolutely. Pppooositively. NNNNOOOO ROOOOOMS AVAILABLE. I would say we will have some openings about the time that all the gold in the Klondike has been mined. Can I help you with anything else? If not, move along."

The man had already left. He must have gotten the message. I felt bad for him not having a place to

The Klondike Gold Rush

stay. The clerk clearly didn't. This must be something that happened quite a bit.

I didn't even bother to ask for a room. I noticed that the clerk had a glass of water on the counter. It looked like a good place to relax, so I slipped into the glass. From there, I would be able to see everything that happened in the hotel lobby. Maybe I would spot someone to travel with. I waited and waited.

A while later, a man rang the bell at the front desk. The clerk came out of the back room. "I'm sorry. We don't have any rooms available," he said in a bored tone.

"Good afternoon, sir. I will not be needing a room from you today." The man spoke with a funny accent. "Instead, I am here to make you a very valuable offer."

My ears perked up at that—so did the clerk's. "What kind of offer?"

"First, let me introduce myself. My name is Count Carbonneau. I represent several fine champagne companies from my home town of Paris, France." That explained his strange accent. "I have a large shipment of fine champagnes scheduled to arrive at the end of the month right here in Dyea."

The clerk was starting to lose interest. "So, what's that got to do with me? What is the offer?"

"If you pre-order your champagne today, I will offer it to you at half the retail price. If you buy a case now, you will be able to double your investment by selling it to your customers at full price when it arrives."

"I don't know…" said the clerk. "We don't really have a big demand for champagne here."

Carbonneau was not discouraged. "Of course not! No one in Dyea has yet tasted the fine champagne of the companies I represent. The best in the world, some say. A smart young man like yourself would find this an excellent investment."

The clerk remained silent as he thought about the offer, but the charming salesman just kept talking. "Imagine this. In just a few short weeks, men will be returning from the Klondike. They will have so much gold, they won't know what to spend it all on. At least not until you offer them a lovely bottle of world-class champagne. Viola! You will have made your money back and then some."

"Alright," said the clerk. "Put me down for a case."

Carbonneau smiled and pulled out a small record book. "Of course, fine sir. Now, I forget to mention…because of the special nature of this offer, I will require full payment in advance."

The clerk made his payment and Carbonneau left. He was headed out to take more orders. For a moment, I wondered if it had been a good idea for the clerk to pay him in advance.

I swam to the top of the water glass. I wanted to get out of there before the clerk took a big drink and I went with it. The heat from the fireplace warmed me up. I became so warm that I was no longer liquid. I floated up out of the glass and through the door.

I was back on the street and trying to decide what to do next. "Last pack horse! No more shipments for two weeks!" The horseman was still at it. "Here's the last horse for sale in all of Dyea. Selling to the highest bidder."

The horse was very sad looking. He was skin and bones, with matted fur. He appeared to be blind in one eye and walked with a bit of a limp. This horse would never make it over the mountain! He looked like he was barely standing.

"I'll give you six hundred and fifty," said a man at the front of the crowd.

"Seven hundred!" yelled another.

This excited the horse owner. "Do I hear seven twenty-five?" A man in the back raised his hand, signaling that he would pay that price.

"Alright then! Seven fifty, anyone?" The original bidder waved his hand.

"Okay…seven fifty. Going once, going twice—"

"Eight hundred!" shouted a newcomer to the crowd.

Eight hundred dollars–for a pitiful specimen of an animal! Now I understand what Grandpa meant when he talked about the law of supply and demand. The higher the demand; the higher the price. The lower the supply; the higher the price. In this case, both supply and demand were working together to make sky-high prices.

The man paid his eight hundred dollars and left with his horse. People jeered at him as he walked by. I think they were just jealous that they hadn't been able to buy the old horse.

I remembered the kind words and happy faces that I had seen on the ship. What had happened? The kind words had been replaced with shouting and rude remarks. The happy faces were now scowls and frowns.

I saw Charles, the man who had been rude to Belinda, walking down the street talking to another man. "I'm going back to Seattle," he said. "This is no place for a civilized person." As it turned out, he wasn't the only one. Many people didn't even attempt to make it up the mountain once they realized how difficult it would be. They just took their losses and headed home. I was the first to admit that things were difficult, but I wasn't ready to go home just yet. I would not give up. I was ready to cross the mountain.

The Klondike Gold Rush

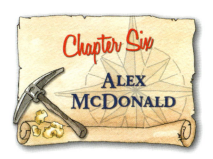

Chapter Six
Alex McDonald

I still hadn't found someone to travel over the mountain with. Thankfully, I ended up amidst the local native tribe. I had heard that the natives were packing goods over the mountains for the stampeders. Maybe, I would find someone to travel with there.

The natives lived in several small villages just outside of Dyea. The townsfolk called them the Chilkoot Indians. In fact, the path through the mountains was called the Chilkoot Pass. The Chilkoots had controlled the pass for years. They had become experts at packing goods over the mountain to trade with the tribes on the other side.

Now, their services were in high demand. What had once cost only twelve cents per pound was now up as high as forty cents. Doesn't sound like much, does it? You have to remember that it cost forty cents per pound. The Canadian government required each person to bring a year's worth of supplies, which weighed about two thousand pounds. Two thousand pounds times forty cents is eight hundred dollars. At that time, eight hundred dollars was a lot of money!

Many people chose not to hire the Chilkoots. It was just too costly. Still, some did hire them.

I met one such man while I was at the village. His name was Alex McDonald. He was a large man, both tall and wide. He looked quite different from the men of the Chilkoot tribe. The Chilkoots were a small people. Their tough, compact bodies were perfect for squeezing through the narrow mountain pass with heavy packs on their backs.

Mr. McDonald was soft-spoken. He did prove, however, to be a shrewd businessman. He was able to negotiate a good price, only twenty-eight cents per pound. The only thing that couldn't be agreed upon was the matter of Sundays.

The Chilkoots refused to work for anyone, even themselves, on Sundays. They were devout Christians who used the day for worship and rest. Mr. McDonald was concerned about the time that would be lost on Sundays. He was anxious to get his goods up and over the mountain as quickly as possible. He even offered to pay double to those willing to work on Sunday.

The Chilkoots wouldn't budge. They would not work on Sunday. They assured Mr. McDonald that they would make better time than anyone else, even those using packhorses. After all, they had been making this trip for generations.

This seemed to satisfy Mr. McDonald. He paid a down payment and left to prepare his things. I went with him, riding on the side of his hat.

I liked Alex McDonald. He wasn't rude or arrogant like so many of the other stampeders I had met. He was smart, too. I could tell by the way he was able to make such a good deal with the Chilkoot packers. He would make a good man to travel with. I decided to join him for the perilous journey through the Chilkoot Pass. Not burdened with supplies, I expected that we would make good time.

Alex wore many layers of clothing, including the heaviest wool socks I had ever seen. He topped it all

The Klondike Gold Rush

off with a fur coat and moccasins. He had purchased these handmade items from the women of the Chilkoot tribe. All this made him very prepared for the bitter cold of the mountain pass. I didn't think he would lose any fingers or toes to frostbite as some had.

Early the next morning, we began our journey through the Coast Mountains. The Chilkoot Pass was very narrow, with deep snowdrifts on both sides. Alex carried only enough food for the journey and a tent to sleep in. The trail was full of people. In some areas, it became so narrow and crowded that there was a single-file line as far as the eye could see.

I was happy to be nestled in the fur of Alex's coat. I was able to stay warm, but still see what was going on. We would be traveling this way for many days, so I wanted to be comfortable. It would be a short trip compared to what others would be making. Many men made multiple trips up and down the mountain, hauling their supplies in sections since they could not afford to hire anyone to pack it for them.

It wasn't long before we started meeting people traveling the opposite direction of us. They had decided not to continue on the dangerous trip, but return back to Dyea and give up. Each one had a different reason for giving up. All day, we listened to the chorus of excuses.

"Too steep."

"Too cold."

"Too crowded."

"Too far."

Just when we thought we had heard it all, a man told us, "I've eaten my shoes and now my feet are cold."

What?!? He ate his shoes? I really wanted to hear about that. Alex must have been curious, too. He paused long enough to hear the man's story. It proved to be quite interesting.

His name was Bishop Isaac Stringer. He was a missionary from Ontario. "I've been living in the Klondike for months, spreading the good news of Jesus Christ," he said. "I've been all over the territory, from the native tribes to the mining camps."

"So, how is it you came to eat your boots, Bishop?" Alex asked.

"I was headed back through the pass, headed to Skagway. I've heard that there's a rascally scoundrel there that goes by the name of Soapy Smith. I had planned on sharing the story of Jesus with him."

Soapy Smith! Bishop Stringer was either a very brave man or a very silly one. I had a feeling he didn't know what he was getting himself into with old Soapy.

He continued his story, "Well, the snow got so heavy, I couldn't see a thing. I somehow got off the trail and was unable to search for the trail because of the snow. I found a small overhang for shelter and ended up being stuck there for several days."

Alex was starting to get antsy. He was losing valuable time on the trail. The man's story was taking longer than expected. He spoke up. "A blizzard...how terrible. How did you end up eating your boots?"

"I didn't have enough food in my pack to last me. I started to get pretty hungry, so I prayed to the good Lord. I said, 'Lord, send me some food to eat.' Then I realized it. My boots were made of sealskin. Surely I could eat them! So I pulled out my little soup pot and boiled those boots 'til I could chew them."

Yuck! I sure didn't like the sound of this story. Now, I was thinking that maybe we shouldn't have stopped to hear it. I hoped that we didn't get stuck in a blizzard. I'd hate for Alex to have to eat his boots. I was glad to be a water molecule since I don't need food to live.

"How did they taste?" Alex asked.

Bishop Stringer paused to think. "Well, I guess they were the best tasting boots I've ever eaten. Of course, I hope I never have to compare it to another pair."

Alex laughed. It was time for us to be going, but first Alex opened up his pack. He rustled through

it and pulled out a pair of moccasins. He gave them to the bishop, who still wore nothing but several pairs of socks and bark tied to the bottom of his feet.

The bishop was very grateful. "May God bless you for your kindness, sir. I thank you."

With that, we were on our way, leaving behind the boot-eating bishop. I turned back to watch him walk away. I shivered as I wondered if something so terrible might happen to us. What danger might wait for us further up the trail?

Chapter Seven
THE GOLDEN STAIRCASE

The Chilkoot Pass was thirty-three miles in length. There were several places along the trail that travelers had set up as rest points. One such place was called Sheep Camp.

I'm not sure why the camp was called Sheep Camp. Maybe the name was chosen because all the people milling around looked like lost sheep. No matter what they looked like, there were a lot of people there—around fifteen hundred.

The talk around the campfires that night was full of Klondike stories. There were stories of gold nuggets the size of baseballs, grizzly bear attacks, and deadly avalanches. It was hard to tell which stories were true and which ones were just tall tales.

Alex told everyone about the bishop who ate his boots. Some of them found it hard to believe. Others thought it seemed like a true story. One woman saw it as a sign of hope.

"Perhaps if that bishop could survive something so awful, then my son is still out there." The woman speaking looked to be in her mid-fifties.

"What happened to your son, ma'am?" Alex asked politely.

"Missing. Told me he was going on a trip and didn't ever come back. I heard he was out in the Klondike mining a claim, and I intend to find him." A tear rolled down her cheek.

"I'm so sorry," said Alex. "What is your son's name? Maybe if I run into him, I'll tell him you are looking for him."

"George. George DeGraf. He's a good boy, you know. Only twenty-three. I'm sure he'll turn up."

Some of the other men told her to go home. It was just too risky for her to be traveling alone. George could be anywhere, they told her.

"You might as well give up trying to stop me," she told them. "I'm not giving up. I'll find my George

THE GOLDEN STAIRCASE

if it means going to the North Pole." She stood up and stomped away.

"She's too stubborn for her own good," one of the men said.

Alex nodded, but said, "A mother's love is a hard thing to understand."

The men all agreed. "I'll tell you what is hard to understand," said one younger fellow. "Salesmen!"

"Salesmen? What do you mean?"

"I ordered a case of champagne from a salesman while I was in Dyea. I thought I might want it to celebrate when I strike gold. Well, it was supposed to arrive in a few days. It never came. Boy, was I mad."

"Well, at least you didn't lose any money like you could have if you paid in advance," said Alex.

The man sighed. "I did pay in advance. I had to pay up front to get the discount. I figured the guy was trustworthy. He was a French count!"

Someone snickered. "You mean Carbonneau? He's not a count! When I saw him in town, I knew it meant trouble. He was my barber back in Montreal. I heard him telling everyone he was a count. I figured he was up to something."

"You can say that again. I wasn't the only one he stiffed. That rogue sold cases to five of the guys at my poker table. Didn't deliver the first bottle."

Carbonneau! He was the man I had seen at the hotel. I knew that the clerk shouldn't have paid him in advance. It just didn't seem right. Now I knew why.

Alex stood up from the campfire. "Well, boys, at least you learned a valuable lesson. You shouldn't trust anybody out here. Goodnight." He walked away with me on his sleeve. We would need a good night's rest. Tomorrow we would face one of the biggest challenges of our journey.

Alex awoke early the next morning and wasted no time getting packed up and ready to go. I settled down on the inside of his hood. I wanted to stay as warm as possible today. If everything went as planned, we would reach the top of the mountain today.

The last half-mile up was very steep. So steep, in fact, that the men had carved a staircase in the ice. It helped a little, but travel was still very hard.

Men held onto a strong cable as they climbed the stairs. We climbed stair after stair after stair. I counted as we went up the mountain.

"Sixty-six, sixty-seven…"

This treacherous section of the trail had come to be called "The Golden Staircase." Everyone knew if they could just get through this rough spot, they would be much closer to the gold.

"One hundred and nineteen, one hundred and twenty…" I kept counting.

A brave journalist had set up his camera at the bottom of the stairs. It was many months later before

I got to see the picture he had taken. It was quite amazing! All those men, in a straight line, walking up the mountain was quite a sight to see.

"Three hundred sixty, three hundred sixty-one…" I wasn't sure how much higher I could count.

I was lucky to get to ride in Alex's coat. No one else was as fortunate. The hard work of traveling all those steps was made worse by the loads they were carrying.

"Five hundred fifty-six, five hundred fifty-seven…"

Some men threw things out of their packs that they didn't need. They were willing to do anything to get rid of some extra weight. Other men collected the cast-offs and hauled them back down the mountain to sell to other stampeders!

"Seven hundred sixty-nine, seven hundred seventy…"

I had never seen so many steps in all my life. Now I knew why all the packhorses had been left further down the trail. No animal would ever make it up this dangerous trail. The animals were also collected and sold again back in Dyea.

THE GOLDEN STAIRCASE

"Nine hundred ninety-nine, one thousand!" We had reached the one thousandth stair. Alex was breathing heavily and barely trudging along. I wondered how many steps could be left.

I caught a glimpse of the Canadian flag. It waved proudly at the top of the summit. Soon we would be passing from Alaska into the great country of Canada.

"Twelve hundred, twelve hundred and one…"

The line had slowed down now. Many men were putting their loads at the top of the mountain and turning around. They still had to go back and get the rest of their things. (One man working alone had to make thirty trips to get all of the necessary supplies up the mountain.)

"One thousand four hundred ninety-nine, one thousand five hundred!" We had reached the top of the summit. There were fifteen hundred stairs in the Golden Staircase. Alex stepped to the side, out of the way of the other men, and sat down to rest. He was exhausted from the long journey.

The Canadian police inspected the loads of those who were ready to cross into Canada. They had to be sure that each man carried his year's worth of supplies. They wanted to be sure that no one would get stuck in the harsh Klondike and starve. The government knew that if thousands of people went in without the adequate supplies that they might steal or kill to get the food of those who did have what they needed.

    I felt a great sense of accomplishment. We had conquered the Golden Staircase. I knew that many would not be able to make this grueling journey. Many would simply turn around and go back home. It was just too difficult and dangerous. I didn't blame them. I hoped that things would be easier now. Something told me, though, that we still faced a long journey. Our gold still seemed so far away.

The Klondike Gold Rush

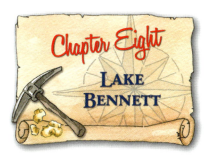

Chapter Eight
Lake Bennett

After we entered Canada, we still had to face the trip down the other side of Chilkoot Pass. It was difficult, but still not as tough as going up had been. It also helped to know that we had conquered the Golden Staircase. Now it felt like we could do anything we put our minds to.

The next day, we were walking along the trail when we heard something strange. It was a loud roar that seemed to shake the entire mountains. The trees even quivered at the sound.

Someone shouted the word we had all been dreading, "Avalanche!" Everyone ran around in a panic. There was no safe place to go. I held onto Alex as tight as I could and hoped for the best.

Soon, the roar went silent. The trees stood still. The avalanche never came.

"It must have been on the other side," said Alex as we got back onto the trail.

He was right. News of the avalanche spread quickly through the Pass. "Sixty stampeders gone," we were told. "A real tragedy."

At the campfire that night, we heard the rest of the story. "The Indians knew it was coming. The Chilkoot packers refused to carry their loads. 'Not today. Weather bad. Snow will come down the mountain.' They waited at the base of the mountain and watched as everyone started up the Pass," a man said.

"Did anyone listen to them?" Alex asked.

"Oh, a few did. Women mostly," replied the man. "Most didn't want to lose a day on the trail. How could those Chilkoot know what was coming? I wouldn't have believed them either."

I shivered at the thought of so many lives lost. Was someone I had met among them? Alex and I had missed the avalanche by only a day. Alex could have been among the dead. I would have been buried deep and frozen under all that snow and ice. It might have been months before it thawed enough for me to get out. It was something I didn't want to think about.

You can bet I was glad when we finally came to the end of Chilkoot Pass. I would be happy to never see that trail again. I was happy that we had made it out without a mishap.

At the base of the trail was Lake Bennett. It was truly a beautiful sight, even though it was frozen solid. The frozen lake had brought travel to a halt for most of the stampeders. They were camped out around the lake, waiting for the first sign of thaw.

Alex made camp on the outer edge of the tents. Next to us were a husband and wife who were African-American. Originally from the Deep South, they were living in Seattle when they heard about the Gold Rush.

"My name's Charles Hunter, and this here is my wife Lucille," said the young man.

"Nice to meet you both," replied Alex.

As Charles and Alex talked, I looked at Lucille. Like her husband, she looked very young. She wore a fur pouch across the front of her body. I wondered what special cargo she carried in there.

"I don't know how you do it, Mr. McDonald, travelin' without a woman. I couldn't make it without my sweet Lucille here. She's the best cook in the Klondike, I tell you," Charles said.

Alex laughed. "Well, maybe I'll find me a fine lady at Dawson City. Until then, I'll just have to make do."

Lucille was busy stirring something in a pot over the campfire. She smiled at her husband's kind words. Then, suddenly, a little squeak came from the direction of the fur pouch.

"Did you hear that?" Alex asked.

"Oh, that? Why that's our little bundle of joy!" Charles said. "Lucille gave birth to that precious baby girl just a few days ago."

A baby! I couldn't believe it. Lucille Hunter had given birth to a baby all the way out here, without a doctor or anyone at all to help her. It was a miracle.

Alex was in awe. "You are one tough woman, ma'am."

Lucille smiled. Charles started talking again. "Tough! Why, she's the toughest woman in the Klondike, I'd wager! Not to mention that she's only nineteen. I've got a jewel in that woman. A jewel. 'Charles,' she told me. 'I want to find a place where our little baby won't be looked down on because of the color of her skin.' So we are headed to Dawson City. You can mine a claim whether you are black, white, or purple, and that's what we intend to do. The folks up this way don't act nothing like they do back South."

"Where is your boat?" Alex asked. "Have you started building it yet?"

Charles grinned and leaned towards Alex. He whispered, "We don't need no boat. I made a deal with the natives. They're gonna take me and Lucille across the ice with their dog sleds. Cost me a pretty penny, but we're gonna to get there faster than everyone sitting around here waitin' for the ice to melt."

"Dog sleds!" said Alex. "Of course! I only wish I had thought of it."

"Now, that, sir, I am sorry about. I wish there was enough to go around, I truly do. Why, I'd trade you our dog team if it weren't for Lucille and the little one. We need to get to Dawson City soon so we can take good care of the baby. We're heading out tomorrow."

"Well, then, good luck," said Alex. "I wish you all well."

I was sad the next morning to see the Hunters leave with their dog team. I thought about going with them, but I had traveled so far with Mr. Alex McDonald. It just wouldn't seem right to abandon him now.

LAKE BENNETT

The next day, Alex began sawing trees so he could begin building his boat. I was too small to be much help, so I traveled around camp to see what else was going on. (Well, I wish I could say I chose to do this. The fact is, I was frozen solid to the coat of a stray dog that had wondered up to the camp the night before.)

Everywhere I went someone was building a boat. The men would need the boats to travel the rest of the way to Dawson City. It was nearly five hundred miles by way of the Yukon River.

There were nearly as many kinds of boats as there were people. Only a very few of the stampeders had ever built a boat before. Some of them had never built anything, much less a boat. A few had the good sense to at least study up on boat building back in Seattle before traveling all this way.

Some people had brought tools along to build their boats, just like the clerk at the general store back in Seattle had said to do. Others had brought nothing to build with. Even worse, some had thrown their heavy tools out while trekking up the Golden Staircase. Boy, they were mad at themselves now!

There were big boats and small boats, tall boats and short boats. Boats with sails and boats without sails. Boats, boats, boats.

Alex took his time building our boat. When it was finished, I thought it was a dandy. It looked roomy enough to carry everything we needed and sturdy enough, too. Now all we had to do was wait for the ice to melt.

We waited and waited and waited. For weeks, we waited for the ice to melt. It wasn't long before the campers started to go stir-crazy. Everyone was anxious to get to Dawson City and stake their claim.

I thought they should consider themselves lucky. At least they weren't frozen solid like poor Munford here. The only time I melted down enough to move around was when Alex got close to the campfire. I was more ready than anyone for spring to come and melt all of the ice, including me.

When the ice began to thin, everyone started to pack up their camps. The time was coming near.

Chapter Nine
THE WHITEHORSE RAPIDS

"Hurry! Come quick! The ice! It's melted!" an overjoyed stampeder ran through the camps yelling at the top of his lungs.

Finally. I couldn't wait to get into Alex's boat and head into the lake and down the Yukon River. I had about all the sitting around I could stand. At least I had thawed out enough to move around now.

When he heard the news, Alex didn't move. What was the matter with him? The campers around us were in frenzy, packing up a few last-minute things. They were tripping over each other as they ran to the lake.

Alex just sat at his campfire. He sipped a cup of coffee he had heated up earlier.

"Come on, Alex! Let's go!" I waved and pointed, trying to get his attention. "Didn't you hear? The ice has melted."

I jumped up and down. "ICE! NO MORE ICE!" I shouted as loudly as I could.

He just sat there and watched everyone rush to the water. Finally, I sat down with a frown. I guess we would just keep waiting. We were going to be the last ones to get to Dawson City. I just knew it.

After I was done feeling sorry for myself, I headed down to the edge of Lake Bennett. (I've gotten pretty good at getting close enough to the fire to evaporate so I can move around easily.) Alex's bad attitude didn't have to stop me from the fun of watching the other campers leave on their boats. It was something to do instead of all the waiting I had been doing.

When I got to the water, I was surprised at what I saw. Most of the ice had melted, but not all of it. There were huge chunks of ice still floating around in the water.

Spending much of my time as ice myself, I knew better than anyone how dangerous ice could be. A big slab of ice like that could rip one of the little boats right down the middle. I would have warned someone, but it was already too late.

Many of the campers, after seeing the ice still left in the water, had turned around and went back to camp. Not everyone was so wise. Anxious to get to the gold, a few brave souls went ahead and launched their boats into the icy water. They must have thought they could just steer around the ice.

It turned out to be a foolish thing to do. The ice began to ram the sides of the boats. The ice punctured even the strongest boats. Some boats managed to make it back to shore before completely sinking. Some weren't so lucky. It was fortunate that so many campers were standing around looking for something to do, because they were quick to pull the soaked stampeders from the water.

The survivors were unhappy. They had lost all of their supplies and the boat they had worked so hard to build. Most just turned around and went back home. It seemed too daunting a task to start over this late in the journey.

I headed back to camp. I guess I owed Alex an apology. He had been right not to rush out into the water. His patience had paid off. I was glad that our boat wasn't sitting at the bottom of the lake, our hopes and dreams sunk with it.

It was several more days before the ice melted completely. No one wanted to rush getting into the water this time. Images of sinking boats still loomed large in their minds.

It was May 29, 1898, when the lake was finally free of all signs of ice. This time, Alex didn't waste anytime launching his boat. Neither did anyone else.

Nearly a thousand boats set sail over the next few days. I already told you about the different shapes and sizes of boats. What a sight the boats were as they headed to Dawson City!

Alex's boat floated like a dream. It even withstood the occasional bump from a boat that came too close to ours. He used oars he had made to guide us downstream.

Our old campsite wasn't even out of view when the men on the boat next to us started to shout. "Help! Help! We're taking on water!" I looked over at their boat. Sure enough, the boat was sinking lower and lower as the men panicked. "Someone! Please! What do we do?"

There was nothing we could do from where we were, at least not fast enough to save the men. "Jump overboard!" shouted Alex.

The men looked horrified, but soon did what he said. Folks on another nearby boat pulled the men out of the water. I breathed a sigh of relief when I saw that they were all still alive. I hoped that would be all of our excitement for the day.

My hopes were dashed when I saw another boat sinking further downstream, then another and another. Many of those inexperienced in boat building had built boats that were not water-worthy. It was a sad sight to see all that hard work quite literally going under.

Our trip down the Yukon River took nearly three weeks. It was mostly uneventful, except for the rapids. We would encounter these every few days. Do you know what a rapid is? A rapid is formed when a river gets more narrow, steep, or shallow. This causes the water to move quickly. It moves so fast that it appears to be white in color. Rapids can be very dangerous.

Some of the rapids on the Yukon River were not anything to get worked up about. Others required some careful steering to get through safely. The Whitehorse Rapids wasn't either one of these. They were the worst we had seen. Being a water molecule, rapids are an adventure for me. All that gravity pulling us water molecules along, dashing us into the rocks, is kind of like a roller coaster. It can be really exciting to be down there in the midst of it.

The Whitehorse Rapids

Riding in a boat through the rapids was a little different. It was scary for everyone because the boat could flip over. The rapids can also slam the boat into rocks, causing it to break. Most of the stampeders pulled their boats out of the water when they got to the Whitehorse Rapids. They pulled their boats with ropes across dry land until they had safely passed the rapids. It was just too risky to attempt going through it, especially since the boats were built by amateurs.

Up until now, Alex had made good, safe decisions. I knew he would pull our boat out and go around the rapids. It was the safe thing to do. We could lose everything if he didn't.

Boy, was I surprised when Alex just steered the boat straight into the rapids! Maybe he decided he didn't want to lose any more time by going around them. Maybe he thought his boat was sturdier than everyone else's.

What a ride! Up and down, side to side. Water splashed over the edges and rolled into the boat. Alex steered us the best that he could. I closed my eyes and held on. "Whhhooooaa!" I yelled as our boat rocked in the waves.

    I didn't open my eyes until I heard men cheering. I peeked out of the corner of my eye. Men stood along the banks clapping and cheering. What were they so happy about?

    I opened both eyes wide. The men were cheering for us. We had made it! We had survived the Whitehorse Rapids. Alex let out a sigh of relief and sat down. It had been a gamble, but we had won.

    Only a very few stampeders were brave enough to face those rapids head on. Some of them

The Whitehorse Rapids

didn't make it through. Their boats were crushed into pieces and left on the banks of the Yukon. A few even drowned in the waters.

I have never felt such a sense of relief as when I caught my first glimpse of Dawson City. I knew that the days of swindlers named Soapy, deadly avalanches, and swirling rapids were behind me, at least for now.

"Yippee!" I'd made it. This was where the first gold of the rush had been found. Here, so many would make their fortunes. I had arrived at Dawson City.

The Klondike Gold Rush

Chapter Ten
Dawson City

The locals didn't call Dawson City by its full name. Instead, they called it "Dawson" for short. Dawson was just another sleepy, rural town before the Gold Rush. Then a man named George Cormack discovered gold in a creek near the city. He filed his gold claim in August 1896. It was months before news of the gold got out.

After the *Portland*, laden with gold, arrived in Seattle, gold prospectors started pouring in from all over the world. (A prospector is someone who tries to make their living by looking for minerals such as gold.) Dawson grew so quickly that no one had time to build any buildings. Many of the stampeders took to calling Dawson a "tent town." As far as you could see, tents were set up as residences and businesses.

The Klondike Gold Rush

The streets of Dawson were very primitive. They were made of dirt. Because of the wet weather, the streets were just pure mud most of the time. Even so, the mud didn't seem to slow down anyone with gold fever.

You've heard me mention gold fever before. I thought maybe I should explain it a little better. Gold fever isn't an actual physical disease. It was the condition of people who were wanting gold. It was an overwhelming desire to make it rich by finding gold.

Pretty much everyone in Dawson had gold fever. What else would cause a person to come all the way from Seattle, across the Coast Mountains, and then five hundred miles down the Yukon River? It was uncontrollable.

For those who made it all the way to Dawson, the gold fever only got worse. The folks who had staked some of the original claims were still living in Dawson. They were filthy rich! They wore the fanciest clothes and had all kinds of nice things.

Merchants stood right in the streets and sold their goods. Jewelry, furs, guns…the finest goods imported from the United States and Europe. The new prospectors practically drooled at the sight of so much wealth. They were more determined than ever to get some gold of their own.

The people of Dawson were glad to see all the new prospectors coming to town. It meant more business for them, and some contact with "the Outside," as they called it. The harsh winters of the Klondike cut the people of Dawson off from the outside world. No one could come and go from the town.

The wealthy were willing to pay any price for news from the States. Prospectors who had wrapped their goods in newspaper to pack them for the journey were fortunate. They could sell the old papers for several dollars a piece! Some of them were even a year old, but it didn't matter.

I figured with all that gold around town that there would be a crime problem. I half expected old Soapy Smith to come around the corner at any moment. He never did.

I didn't see much crime, but I did see the Northwest Mounted Police. These men on their horses patrolled Dawson at all hours. They did this for the same reason they required everyone to bring in a year's worth of supplies. They wanted everyone to be safe.

The one thing the Mounties, as they were called, couldn't control was the prices. Like the price of the newspapers, many things in Dawson were not affordable to a normal person. Only the wealthiest miners could afford some of the luxuries.

Something happened to Alex that will give you an idea about what kind of luxuries people wanted.

It all started the first morning we were there. Alex decided he was thirsty. Not just thirsty for anything. He wanted a glass of milk.

What do you do when you want a glass of milk? Just go to the refrigerator and get it? Or, maybe you are out of milk, so you wait for someone to go to the grocery store to get some? Don't you hate having to wait for milk?

Alex really wanted that milk, so he started asking around about where he could get some milk. Everywhere he asked he got the same answer, "Cow Miller."

I thought Cow Miller was a pretty strange name for someone, but no one else seemed to think so. "Oh, you want milk? You need to head on out to Cow Miller's place. He'll get you taken care of if you're willing to pay."

Of course Alex was willing to pay. He wanted some milk! We left our small campsite and headed to Cow Miller's place.

Cow Miller lived in a tent just like everyone else, although it appeared that he was working on building a place to live. He had fenced in a small piece of land. Inside the fence were twenty cows.

Alex was happy to see the cows, because he knew that cows meant milk. Several people were standing around the fence, so Alex asked one of them "Is this where I buy the milk?"

A young lady spoke up, "Yes, sir. We are all just waiting on Cow Miller to return. He's in town picking up some supplies and should be back any moment."

"Alright then," said Alex. "Do any of you know how this man got the name Cow Miller?" Alex must have been wondering the same thing I was.

The lady let out a small giggle. "Because of the cows, of course!"

Alex didn't understand. "Pardon me, ma'am, if I seem confused, but I owned quite a few cows back in the States, and no one ever called me Cow."

One of the men that were there spoke up, "Ol' Miller's the only person in all of Dawson who has cows, and only one of 'em's a milking cow. He's become right popular. Ain't no one had milk since sometime last winter when the last milking cow in Dawson froze to death."

"Well, how did 'Cow' get to Dawson with all

these cows? There's no way he managed to get those things through the Chilkoot Pass."

"You're right about that. He took the rich man's route—boat all the way from Seattle, up the Pacific and down the Yukon River. Took him nearly a year, but he and his cows made it."

Alex was surprised to hear that. "I didn't know you could do that."

The young lady spoke up. "Well, it is terribly expensive. Not to mention that the river freezes up and the boats get stuck. Mr. Miller managed to get through before word of the gold got out. It wasn't as costly then. Speaking of Mr. Miller, there he is!"

Sure enough, there stood a man carrying a load of bottles in one arm. Alex stepped up to introduce himself, "Mr. Miller, my name's Alex McDonald." He extended his hand for a shake.

They shook hands, but Mr. Miller said, "Oh, now, call me Cow. Everyone else in this town does." He laughed.

"I'm guessing you're all here about the milk. I'm afraid I'm already all sold out for today, but you might try back tomorrow. Old Bessie should have a little more milk for us by then. I can hardly milk her fast enough."

Alex frowned. He had really wanted some milk. "Do you know of anywhere else I could buy some milk?"

Cow Miller grinned. "I'm afraid not, Mr. McDonald. If everyone in Dawson had a milk cow, they wouldn't call me Cow, now would they? Just try back tomorrow. Be sure to bring your gold dust, though. The milk's been bringin' about thirty dollars a gallon."

Thirty dollars a gallon! Whoa! The people of Dawson must have really wanted that milk. Alex headed back to town in a sad state. It looked like he wouldn't be getting his milk after all. He wouldn't even go back tomorrow, not at thirty dollars a gallon. It was just too much. Besides, pretty soon we would be heading out of Dawson to look for gold claims. There was no time to waste waiting around for milk.

The Klondike Gold Rush

Chapter Eleven
GOLD DUST

Alex started asking around Dawson about gold claims. He wanted to know as much as he could before he started looking for one of his own. He was pretty disappointed to find that most of the land for many, many miles was already claimed. "Gold for the taking," as the newspapers had said in Seattle, wasn't really true. Most of the good claims were already being worked.

"Your best bet is to head out to a little bunkhouse, about fifteen miles from here. It is near most of the good claims. If you're lucky, you might be able to get a job working someone's claim," someone in town told him.

Ha! I certainly wouldn't be working anyone's claim unless it was my own. I had come all this way to get rich for myself. I didn't do it to work while somebody else gets rich.

I could tell Alex didn't like the sound of that, either. There weren't a lot of choices, though, so we headed out to the bunkhouse. It seemed pretty smart to me that someone had built the bunkhouse all the way out by the mines. It kept people from having to go back to town for everything they needed.

When we arrived, I could tell that the bunkhouse had been freshly built. It also had a food counter where hot meals were served to miners after a long day's work.

Alex stepped up to the counter to inquire about a bunk. He must have wanted a break from the camping life. It would be a good way to meet new people and talk about gold claims. A woman in a pretty apron came out to talk to him.

"I'm sorry, sir, but we are full. We don't even have a blanket left, or I would let you sleep on the floor."

I looked a little closer at the woman. Her voice sounded so familiar. I tried to think of where I had seen her.

Alex was persistent. "Maybe if I could speak to the owner…"

Wait a minute! Now I recognized her. It was Belinda Mulroney. Remember her? She was the woman I had boarded the boat with to head for the Klondike. She must have found herself a job working right here near the mines.

Belinda let out a little sigh. She put her hands on her hips. Her face reminded me of the day on the boat when Charles had insulted her. "Well, sir, I am afraid that you are speaking to the owner. I built this bunkhouse and everything that goes along with it with my own hard-earned money."

Alex seemed impressed. "My apologies, ma'am. It isn't often I meet a hard-working woman like yourself."

Belinda's face softened. "Thank you, sir. I appreciate that. I might be able to find you a spot, if you've packed your own blanket and mattress roll."

"I do have that, ma'am."

"Okay, then. I have some other things to attend to, but my husband will take your money and point you to your place on the floor." She stuck her head into the back room, "Darling? Can you take care of this gentleman? I've got to get back to the kitchen."

Belinda's husband stepped out of the back room. Do you know I fell right off of Alex's sleeve and onto the floor? That is how shocked I was when I saw just who the husband was.

It was "Count" Carbonneau—the "champagne salesman" from Paris. No kidding! If you remember, it turned out that he was really just a Canadian barber turned conman. I couldn't believe he had married

sweet Belinda. I thought that people got married because they loved each other, but in this case, I don't know. I have a feeling that the sly "Count" must have known Belinda was going to make some money.

I wished that Alex could have warned Belinda, but he had never met the man before. Of course he didn't recognize him. Maybe someone else would come along and tell her. I climbed back up onto Alex's sleeve and hoped for the best.

At the meal table that night, Alex started asking about gold claims again. He wanted to know where the best claims were. He wanted a claim for himself.

"It's no use," one of the men said. "There isn't an unclaimed piece of land for miles."

"Surely there's something?" Alex asked.

"Nothing. All these thousands of people flooding into Dawson thinking they're gonna get rich don't know what they've got coming. All the best spots were claimed months ago. There's nothing left. Nothing, I tell you."

Alex kept asking questions. "What about you? Do you have a claim?"

"Me? Well, sort of. I've lived in Dawson all my life. When McCormack staked his claim, I staked a few of my own just like everyone else. I've still got them, but I never found much at all. Now I make my living running errands for the big miners."

Alex didn't hesitate a second. "Sell me your claims then."

The man looked shocked. "What? Are you crazy? I told you. I haven't mined hardly a thing off either one of them."

"I didn't say I'd pay much for them," came Alex's reply. "Whatever you think they're worth, which doesn't sound like much."

"Well, they aren't doing me any good. Fine. It's a deal."

"Okay, then." Alex leaned back in his chair. I couldn't understand why he was so happy. He had just bought some worthless mining claims. He turned to another man at the table. "What about you? What do you do?"

"Don't look at me, mister. I don't have any claims. I just got here. I came all the way from San

Francisco, and for what? There are no claims left and I still haven't been able to find a job."

Alex chewed on his food as he thought. "Are you a hard worker?"

"Yes, sir. I owned my own ranch back in California. Why, I worked from sun up to sun down just trying to turn a profit."

"Okay. You're hired."

The man spit his food out right on his plate. "What?"

Alex smiled. "I said you're hired. You start tomorrow. I want you to work the land I just bought. You can have a percentage of whatever you find."

The man jumped up from the table and shook Alex's hand. "Thank you, sir. Thank you. If there's a speck of gold dust on that land, I'll find it, sir. Just wait and see."

"Excuse me, gentlemen, I just need to sweep under your feet." Belinda came by with a broom.

When she was out of earshot, one of the men leaned over and whispered to Alex. "She's always sweeping this place. Sweep, sweep, sweep. Why do you think that is?"

Alex didn't bother whispering. "I don't know. She likes the place clean?" It made sense to me.

"Shh!!" The man leaned closer. "It's the gold dust. All these miners track in dirt on their boots from the mine. She burns off the dirt and all that's left is gold dust. Rumor has it she makes a hundred dollars a night just from the dirt on the floors."

"Well, I'll be. Smart woman." Alex said.

I noticed that the room was getting warmer and warmer. There were so many people in the small space that it was getting warm quick. Before I knew it, I had evaporated.

Evaporation is when water heats up and turns to steam. When that happens, I get to float around, which is pretty cool. It was time to move on, anyway. Unlike Alex, I wasn't interested in buying gold claims. I just wanted to find some gold of my own. Tomorrow, I would go looking for gold. Until then, I found a nice cozy place on the ceiling of the dining room. As Belinda's customers left for their bunks and the night air came into the room, I condensed back into a regular water drop. I would relax until the next morning, when something exciting was sure to happen.

The Klondike Gold Rush

Chapter Twelve
PANNING FOR GOLD

It was the next morning when I awoke to someone shaking me. "Munford! Munford! Wake up!"

I rolled over. I didn't want to be bothered. It had been a long week after all.

"Munford! Get up now!"

I tried opening my eyes, but they were just too tired. "Munford! It is a quarter past noon. You have wasted half the day. You'll never find any gold like this."

"Fine, fine." I opened my eyes to find none other than wise, old Grandpa Gilbert. "Grandpa! What are you doing here?'

"Well," said Grandpa, "I hadn't heard from you in a while. I figured I would've gotten word if you had found your gold. I thought you might need some help."

I jumped up. "Thank you so much, Grandpa. How did you get here so fast? Did you take the rich man's route by water? Did you come through the Chilkoot Pass?"

"Goodness, no, Munford. I told you that I am just too old for that kind of nonsense. I took the fastest route around—a rain cloud."

Why hadn't I thought of that? It would have made my trip to Dawson City a lot faster. Of course, I wouldn't have met all the interesting people if I had traveled that way.

Grandpa Gilbert began tapping his foot. "So, what have you been doing? Sleeping? Don't you know that water molecules don't need to sleep?"

I didn't really know what to say. "Um…Well…I know. I was just waiting for the humans to wake up, so I could get started on my plan. Except…I don't really have a plan exactly."

"No plan?!?"

"That's right…No plan."

He twisted his mouth into a funny little frown. I knew just what that meant. He was going to give me a lecture. "Have I taught you nothing, Munford? Always start every day with a plan. One day, you could end up being a great adventurer, just like me. Why, I am famous all over the world for my explorations. You can bet that didn't happen by accident. No sir. I did it by making a plan. You simply must have a plan."

I shrugged. "I know. You're right. I should have had a plan, but you are here now. Help me decide what to do today. Where should I start looking for gold?"

"Let's think about that for a minute," Grandpa said and then proceeded to explain to me a little about gold and where it comes from. "Deep in the earth's mantle, buried under tons and tons of pressure, lie all kinds of different minerals, such as gold, quartz, and silver. The minerals are in liquid form because it is so hot in the mantle. Occasionally, a crack will form in the mantle. The minerals flow up through the crack and cool, causing them to harden."

I interrupted Grandpa. "I don't know. That all sounds pretty complex, Gramps. I don't know where I would even start to look for a crack in the earth's mantle."

Grandpa laughed. "Well, that's just the thing. No one really knows where to look for those. You need to know what happens next, then you will understand what happens to the gold.

"You see, water molecules—just like you and me—rain down on the deposits of gold. This breaks them down into small pieces called nuggets. Then, more water molecules, in the form of rivers and streams, carry the nuggets and bits of gold dust away from the original deposit. So, most prospectors start looking near water to find the gold."

It was all starting to make sense now. "Alright! All we have to do is find another water molecule who helped move the gold. He can tell us where to find the gold!"

"Hang on, Munford. The water molecules that moved this gold are probably long gone by now. They might be half way around the world for all we know. They could be on a beach somewhere taking a vacation. No, that plan won't work. You are going to have to go down to one of the streams and pan for gold just like everybody else around here is doing."

Panning for Gold

He didn't have to tell me twice. I hung near the door of Belinda's bunkhouse. I hoped to catch a swirl of wind that blew when folks came in and out. I wanted to make my way to the nearest stream. Grandpa Gilbert wished me luck as I whooshed out the door.

Two gentlemen were already working the stream where I ended up. It was a pretty good-sized stream, though. I figured they wouldn't mind if I did a little looking of my own. I headed over to their stack of pans. I thought I would borrow one, but there was just one little problem—me.

I was too small to carry the pan to the water. I pushed and pulled and tugged, but with no luck. I just could not get that pan to move for anything. What was I going to do now? I certainly didn't have a plan for this.

The men at the stream were scooping up rocks, dirt, and water in their gold pans. They would then slowly shake the pan back and forth while it was still in the water. Dirt and gravel would float out, but heaver things would stay in the pan. If they were lucky, there would be some gold left among the heavier things.

I jumped into the stream and headed towards them. I hoped they would scoop me up into one of their pans. Maybe then I would be able to spot some gold for myself.

Sure enough, in just a few minutes, one of the men had me in his pan. I looked and looked, but didn't see any signs of gold. I swam out of that pan and into the pan of the other man. There was no gold there, either.

For hours, I went from pan to pan just looking for the smallest hint of gold. It reminded me of the times I watched people fish. They would sit there all day and never get a bite. It took a lot of patience, just like gold panning.

Just when I was about to give up, I spotted a glimmer of something in one of the pans. I swam towards it as fast as I could. There it was. A real gold nugget! Not just any nugget, either. It was a big one.

I grabbed onto the gold, but quickly fell over. The pan was being lifted out of the water. I held on tight.

"Look at this, John!" said the man holding the pan. "I reckon I found us some gold!" He pulled the nugget out of the pan. I hung dangerously from the edge of it.

John came over and let out a yelp. "We're rich!"

Wait a minute! They weren't rich. I was. That gold nugget was mine. I had found it, fair and square. I shouted and shouted. They just kept clapping and cheering.

I was mad now. I had come all the way from Seattle, Washington to find this gold. I had hiked over the very dangerous Chilkoot Pass. I had come five hundred miles down the Yukon River. I had bravely rode through the Whitehorse Rapids. I had looked Soapy Smith straight in the eye, for heaven's sake! The gold was mine. Mine, mine, mine.

None of this mattered to John and his buddy. They held the gold up to get a better look. I tried to keep holding on, but my arms were getting so tired. I fell to the ground with a splash.

I watched in sadness as those dirty scoundrels walked away with my gold.

Chapter Thirteen
Nuggets of Gold

I rested in a cloud under the stars that night, disappointed. I had lost my gold nugget. I just couldn't face Grandpa Gilbert until I had found another one.

I needed a new plan. Grandpa would have been glad to know that I was trying to plan ahead, wouldn't he? I wanted to find a better mining operation, not just a couple of guys panning in the stream. Then I would find my gold.

Grandpa Gilbert had mentioned to me that streams weren't the only places with gold. A lot of gold was also buried in older streambeds. These beds dried up over time and were slowly covered with new dirt and sediment. The only way to get to this gold was to dig it up.

I floated with the wind in search of someone who was digging up gold. I passed a lot of operations panning in the creeks. I even passed a few abandoned claims that people had just given up on and left.

Eventually, I saw an operation that was digging up an old streambed. There were only two men, but they looked like they were working hard. I was interested to see how this kind of mining worked.

I was surprised to find that the man in charge was Charles Hunter. Do you remember Charles? I had met him and his wife, Lucille, back at Lake Bennett. They had beaten me to Dawson because they had rented a team of sled dogs to take them there.

I was excited to see Charles. I soon realized that this was his claim. He wasn't just working for somebody else.

Charles had hired a man to work for him. Lucille and the baby must have been back at their camp, because I didn't see them around. This kind of mining was strenuous work and no place for a small child.

I figured that digging up old streams would be pretty easy. How hard could it be? All you would need is a good shovel and a little elbow grease, right?

I was wrong about that. It turned out to be a little more complex than that. This was the Klondike, after all. The problem was that the ground was frozen solid. A shovel just bounced right off of it. Before any digging could be done, the ground had to be thawed. They would light a fire and let it burn for a while, until the dirt was loose enough to dig. They would put out the fire and dig until they hit frozen ground again.

They would light another fire in the hole they had dug. When the soil had loosened up, they would dig some more. The hole would eventually become a tunnel. These tunnels were called shafts.

When they reached the streambed, they would haul up all the gravel and dirt and put it in a big pile. They would then pan it for gold in a big tub of water. Sometimes they would find some. Sometimes they didn't.

Once they had exhausted one shaft, they would start digging another one. Dig, dig, dig. All day, Charles and his man would dig.

I saw a big tub of water where they panned for gold. Nearby, they kept a small bucket full with the gold they had found. I peeked inside. Sure

enough, inside was a little gold dust, some gold flakes, and a few nuggets. It looked like they were doing pretty well.

I managed to land into the tub where all the gravel and dirt had settled to the bottom. Perhaps they had missed something, anything. I just wanted a small piece of gold to make my grand Klondike adventure worthwhile. Sadly, there was nothing left in the dirt. Not even a speck of gold.

I thought about that bucket of gold nearby. If I could hitch a ride over there, I could just take a small piece for myself. They had plenty! They would never notice. It wouldn't really be stealing. I mean, they had just left that bucket there. They must have meant for someone like me to take some of it.

I was just trying to find a way to get to the bucket, when a woman approached. It was Lucille! She still wore a pouch, but this time I could see a little head sticking out of the top. A little girl smiled and cooed as Charles came up and tossed some gravel in to the tub. Here was my chance. I splashed up onto his glove. Maybe now I could get closer to the bucket of gold.

"There are my two girls," said Charles. He kissed his wife on the cheek.

"I brought you some lunch," said Lucille. "How is it going today?"

Charles smiled. "Pretty good, dear. Pretty good. We have found a lot of dust, and even a few nuggets."

"That's good enough for me, Charles. I don't want to be filthy rich like some of the folk around here. I think too much gold ruins a person." I climbed up the side of the bucket and peered in.

"You're absolutely right, Lucille. Absolutely right," Charles said. "As long as we have each other, that's what I say. I'm already the richest man in the Klondike. Even if we didn't find a scrap of gold, it doesn't matter. I already know what's important. You and our little baby girl."

Lucille hugged her husband. "I love you," she said.

"I love you, Lucille. I love you."

As I debated how to get into the bucket of gold, I couldn't help but smile at those two. I had seen a lot of people on my journey to the Klondike. Selfish, rude, arrogant people. People who didn't care about anyone or anything, just gold. Gold, gold, gold.

The Hunters were different. They cared about each other. Nothing else was as important as their love for each other. The gold was just a way to make a living. They weren't going to let it control them.

Suddenly, it hit me. Here I was, about to steal a piece of gold for myself. What a terrible thing to do! From this sweet little family, no less.

I didn't need any gold. The most valuable part of my journey would never be a big golden nugget.

Of course, that would be nice to have, but I had still enjoyed the experience. The people I had met, good and bad, the scenery, the adventure, and everything else all added up to be pretty worthwhile.

As the warm afternoon sun turned me into steam, I floated through the air over the Hunter's land. I vowed to myself that I would never let gold fever get to me again, and I would never, ever steal gold from anyone. I was a water molecule, after all. What would I do with gold, anyway? I waved goodbye and headed back towards Dawson to find Grandpa Gilbert. I may not have had any gold, but I did have quite a story to tell!

A Note from Grandpa Gilbert

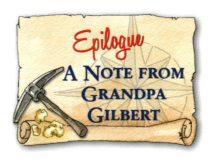

The Klondike Gold Rush had a lasting effect on the Western United States and the Klondike region of Canada. The throngs of stampeders headed to the West Coast aided the development of gateway cities, such as Seattle, San Francisco, and Portland. The purchase of supplies—which by some estimates equaled more than the total amount of gold taken from the Klondike—created a boom of business in what had been a slumping economy.

One hundred thousand people attempted entry into the Klondike during the Gold Rush. Of those hundred thousand, only forty thousand ended up making it there. The ones that didn't make it often settled at various points along the route, aiding in the settlement of Alaska and Canada. The growing number of citizens in the Klondike region itself prompted the Canadian Parliament to declare a separate territory, the Yukon. Alaska became a territory of the United States in 1912, going on to become a state in 1959.

When the stampeders finally arrived, they found that most of the gold had already been claimed. Even so, in 1900, the peak year of gold extraction, over twenty-two million dollars worth of gold was removed from the Klondike region. The majority of this was done by commercial gold operations, not individual miners.

Anna DeGraf traveled all over the Klondike in search of her son, George. She carried her sewing machine the entire way, earning her living by stitching up garments for the prospectors. She never did find George.

Charles and Lucille Hunter managed to stake an early gold claim after arriving safely in Dawson with their dog team. They worked the claim successfully and made a good living for themselves. Even after Charles died, Lucille continued to work the mines until she died in the Yukon at the age of 97.

A Note from Grandpa Gilbert

Belinda Mulroney made a fortune providing room and board for Klondike prospectors. She eventually earned enough money to build the Fairview Hotel. She personally arranged to have huge chandeliers, brass beds, and all the latest luxuries packed over the Chilkoot Pass to outfit her new hotel. The Fairview was a huge hit, only adding to her wealth. She eventually lost most of her fortune to her swindling husband, Count Carbonneau. She managed to earn it back running similar operations at another, smaller gold rush in Nome, Alaska.

Alex McDonald is called the "King of the Klondike." He bought all the claims that he could, and hired others to mine them. He paid his help a percentage of whatever they found. This system helped him to become one of the wealthiest men in the Yukon at the time.

...and the rest is history.

The Klondike Gold Rush

FASCINATING FACTS

- Author Jack London was a prospector during this gold rush. He later went on to write *White Fang* and *The Call of the Wild* which were influenced by experiences during his Klondike days.

- The Canadian Northwest Mounted Police enforced the laws of the land throughout the rush of prospector activity. This helped make the Klondike Gold Rush the most peaceful of this kind in history. The Mounted Police became famous all over the world as a result.

- Most of all the paying claims were staked out within six months of when the first gold nugget was pulled out of Rabbit Creek by George Carmack.

- As many as 2800 people a week passed through Seattle by boat enroute to the Yukon in search of gold.

- An "outfit"—tools, stove, tent, nails, and supplies—to last a year weighed in at a whopping 2000 pounds and cost about $500.

- Twenty thousand prospectors climbed the Chilkook Pass during the winter of 1897. Most made their way up and back down the pass numerous times in order to carry all of their supplies with them.

- After the rush of individual prospectors died down, a railway from Skagway was completed. This was used by commercial mining companies who continued to extract gold for another fifty years.

Author's Note

SHARING THE VISION OF MUNFORD

I met Josh and Cindy Wiggers, the fine folks behind Geography Matters, while I was still in high school. Their kids and I went to church together and were becoming fast friends. It wasn't long before I went to the Wiggers house for a visit. Josh made quite an impression on me. First, he insisted that everyone call him Uncle Josh. Second, every conversation, it seemed, ended up turning into a geography drill. "What is the smallest country in the world? What is the capital of Zambia? What country is located between France and Spain?" Needless to say, all of these questions were a little overwhelming, but I kept going back for more visits and more geography drills.

Uncle Josh began telling me about a vision he had of a character he named Munford. He had first dreamed up the little water molecule many years before in a moment of inspiration while driving on the highway in the rain. Because Munford was water, he could be anywhere at anytime in history. By following his adventures, kids could learn about science, history, and geography. There would be almost no limit to what Munford could do. The only problem was that Uncle Josh hadn't been able to find a writer that was a good match for Munford. He had heard that writing was a hobby of mine, and wanted me to give it a try. I'm not sure exactly why he chose to take a chance on me. I was only a sophomore in high school! He must have liked my sample chapter, though, because he asked me to finish the book (*Munford Meets Lewis and Clark*) and then write others (*The Klondike Gold Rush, The American Revolution*, and more to come…).

It was 2002 when I first set pen to page and wrote Munford's first adventure. Since then, Uncle Josh and the rest of the Wiggers family became like a part of my extended family. Geography Matters has grown and flourished as one of the best homeschooling publishers on the market today. Munford himself has gone through many changes, thanks to multiple revisions, illlustrators, and improvements.

Munford, who is actually a water molecule, is often referred to and portrayed as a water drop. A water drop is actually made of many water molecules, so I took some artistic license by calling him a drop. It is easier to understand and visualize Munford as a drop rather than a teeny, tiny, molecule that cannot be seen with the naked eye.

My hope for Munford is that he will teach your children without them even realizing how much they are learning. Who knows, if they ever have the chance to meet Uncle Josh, or someone like him, perhaps they will be able to answer those pesky geography, history, or science questions with pride.

Munford's Other Adventures

THE AMERICAN REVOLUTION

In this adventure, Munford travels to colonial America and experiences first hand the events leading to the American Revolution. He meets famed American Founding Fathers, such as Samuel Adams, Thomas Jefferson, and George Washington. He joins the Sons of Liberty under cover of night to dump tea into Boston Harbor. He tags along for Paul Revere's most famous ride, and even becomes a part of the Declaration of Independence in a way that you might not expect!

MUNFORD MEETS LEWIS & CLARK

Join him on an epic adventure with Meriwether Lewis and William Clark, as they make their perilous journey in search of the Northwest Passage to the Pacific Ocean. Munford will inspire your children to learn more about the Corps of Discovery and the expedition that changed the face of America.

MORE TO COME ...

Look for more adventures in this exciting series as Munford's journey through time and territory continues around the world.

Other Titles Published by Geography Matters

Cantering the Country by Loree´ Pettit and Dari Mullins

Galloping the Globe by Loree´ Pettit and Dari Mullins

***Trail Guide to...Geography* series** by Cindy Wiggers

Geography Through Art by Sharon Jeffus and Jamie Aramini

***Trail Guide to Learning* curriculum series** by Debbie Strayer & Linda Fowler

Uncle Josh's Outline Map Book by George Wiggers and Hannah Wiggers

Uncle Josh's Outline Map Collection CD-ROM

Lewis and Clark, Hands On by Sharon Jeffus

***Profiles from History* series** by Ashley Wiggers

Laminated Maps

Laminated Outline Maps

Mark-It Timeline of History

Timeline Figures CD-ROMs

And much more . . .

Contact us for our current catalog,
or log on to our website.
Wholesale accounts and affiliates welcome.

(800) 426-4650   www.geomatters.com

About the Author

Jamie Aramini is the author of *Eat Your Way Around the World*, *Geography Through Art* with Sharon Jeffus, and the *Adventures of Munford* series. She graduated co-valedictorian of her high school class and was a Kentucky Governor's Scholar. She is currently raising her two sons, a flock of chickens, and a miniature Schnauzer named Sophie. Her hobbies include organic gardening, cooking, and teaching writing at her local homeschool co-op. Visit www.jamiearamini.com to learn more about Jamie.

About the Illustrator

Emily Lefferts is a homeschool graduate from Sutton, Massachusetts. She is currently studying visual arts with a concentration in illustration at Gordon College. Her courses at Gordon have taken her to Italy where she spent a semester studying art. After graduation, she hopes to continue working as an illustrator. She lives at home with seven siblings, four dogs, and two very patient parents.